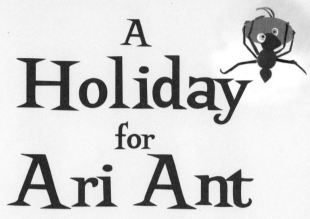

A Holiday for Ari Ant

by Sylvia Rouss

Illustrated by Katherine Janus Kahn

This **PJ BOOK** belongs to

_____

_____

PJ Library®
JEWISH BEDTIME STORIES and SONGS

APPLES & HONEY PRESS

Springfield, NJ ◆ Jerusalem

ri Ant lived on the school playground. He loved watching the children play and laugh, even though he had to be careful of their running feet...

...or scramble out of the way of an oncoming tricycle!

One day, Ari sat with the children under a large shady tree, as they listened to their teacher telling them about the holiday of Lag B'Omer.

"A long, long time ago, the Jewish people weren't allowed to listen to Torah stories," she told them.

"But the children wanted to hear those stories so much, they pretended to go olive picking and took their picnic lunches into the hills! After their picnic, they rested in caves and heard the wonderful stories they loved.

"Soon we will celebrate Lag B'Omer and go on a picnic and listen to stories too, just like those children did so long ago!" said the teacher. Ari couldn't wait.

Later that day, Ari saw two girls having a pretend Lag B'Omer picnic. They spread out a blanket and put plates of food on it. Ari didn't notice the food wasn't real!

The hungry ant crept up and bit into a cookie, but his teeth couldn't grasp its hard slippery surface.
"I'm not sure I like Lag B'Omer!" said Ari, very disappointed.

The next morning, Ari Ant watched closely as some children played in the sandbox, making a cave out of wet sand. They carefully put their dolls inside and whispered stories into the cave opening.

Ari eagerly crawled
inside the cave. He wanted
to hear those stories, too!
But suddenly a big lump of sand
fell on top of him! Ari could hardly
breathe. He scurried away to safety.
"I'm not sure I like Lag B'Omer!"
coughed the sandy little ant.

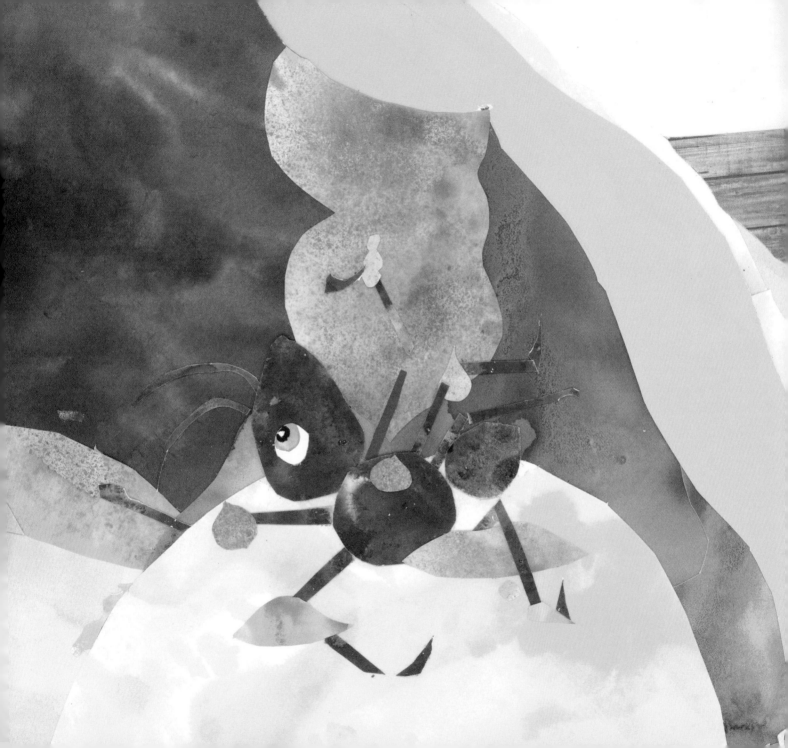

After lunch, Ari watched
the children as they
gathered happily around
an outdoor table.

They were decorating visors
with sparkly sequins for the
picnic! Ari climbed up to
get a closer look...

... and stepped right into a puddle of glue.

Oh no! His feet stuck fast. He had to use all
his strength to pull himself free. "I'm not sure
I like Lag B'Omer!" said the sticky ant.

Back on the ground, Ari
noticed a shiny red sequin.

"I like this sparkly
cap, though!"

He picked it up
and tried it on.

At last the day of the picnic arrived, and Ari Ant was ready to go. In fact, he had been ready and waiting since early morning!

At noon, the children raced outside, wearing sparkly visors and carrying their picnic baskets.

Ari
quickly
jumped
onto a
boy's
shoe
and
held
on
tight
as
the
children
followed
their teachers through
the school gate and into the nearby park.

In the distance, Ari saw a small hill. As the children ran up it, Ari lost his grip.

"Wait for me!" he panted, trying to keep up.

Ari huffed and puffed as he climbed the hill.
I hope I don't miss all the fun! he thought.
At last, he reached the top. The children
were helping to open a large umbrella.

"Wow!" exclaimed Ari. "It looks just
like a cave!"

The teacher unfolded a big blanket
and laid it on the ground. Ari
scrambled to find a safe place
to sit. What a lunch! There
were watermelon slices, hotdogs,
brownies and grapes.

Crumbs fell everywhere, along with drops of watermelon juice. Ari didn't know what to try first. Later, the children listened to Torah stories. Ari sighed happily. He loved that part!

The sun began to set, and the children's parents arrived. Some were carrying wood for a bonfire.

Under the evening sky, as the flames gently shimmered,
Ari Ant rubbed his full tummy and exclaimed,
"I love Lag B'Omer!
It's the perfect
holiday for me!"

APPLES & HONEY PRESS

An imprint of Behrman House and Gefen Publishing House
Behrman House, 11 Edison Place, Springfield, New Jersey 07081
Gefen Publishing House Ltd., 6 Hatzvi Street, Jerusalem 94386, Israel
www.applesandhoneypress.com

ISBN 978-1-68115-507-4

Library of Congress Cataloging-in-Publication Data
Rouss, Sylvia A.
A holiday for Ari Ant / by Sylvia Rouss ; Illustrated by Katherine Janus Kahn.
pages cm

Summary: After hearing about Lag B'Omer, Ari the playground ant is excited to join a group of nursery school
children in their celebration but the children's playtime activities leading up to the big day have Ari questioning
whether it is a good holiday for an ant.

ISBN 978-1-68115-507-4

[1. Lag b'Omer--Fiction. 2. Judaism--Customs and practices--Fiction. 3. Jews--United States--Fiction. 4. Ants--
Fiction.] I. Kahn, Katherine, illustrator. II. Title.

PZ7.R7622Hol 2016
[E]--dc23
2014044639

Design by Benjie Herskowitz, Etc. Studios
Printed in China
1 3 5 7 9 8 6 4 2

041627.5K1/B0810/A4